For Sandra & Terry
with much love
Jo Ridey

The Feminine
by Richard Kehl

A Star & Elephant Book

Green Tiger Press

La Jolla · London

1986

INTRODUCTION

This work is an essay on the feminine, composed almost entirely of pictures.

Looking at it, one enters a special world, a world in which meaning is revealed by the interplay of images, a world in which the arrangement of the images is as important as the images themselves.

What sparked the creation of this work was the realization that something magical and unexpected happens when two images are placed side by side. There is "something in between" that flourishes in the shadows and margins. A new language of pictures echoes from these interstices, a language beyond analysis. The logic of the juxtapositions is especially "feminine" in nature: the inner eye sees that the pictures are just right together, and the satisfied viewer needs not ask why. Neither the images in this book nor the few words—these included—try to explain or analyze the feminine. Rather, they embody it. Taken together, the elements of this book lead the viewer toward a larger, more intuitive, less verbal, yet strangely more precise understanding.

To enjoy the book in its own terms, one must allow free play of one's feminine qualities: receptivity, quietude, a close connection to the rhythm of being, a sense of wholeness, a preference for the instinctive, a trust in the invisible, and a willingness to accept things without naming, categorizing, or dissecting them.

By now, it should be obvious that *The Feminine* is not exclusively about woman. It is about a principle of creation, of which woman is but one manifestation. This feminine spirit exists not just in woman, but in every man as well. It is the mysterious source of power that points us to our deepest selves, and makes us complete. To be feminine is to be porous, understanding, attentive.

We hope that this book will bring about a new awareness of the feminine quality that is in all of us.

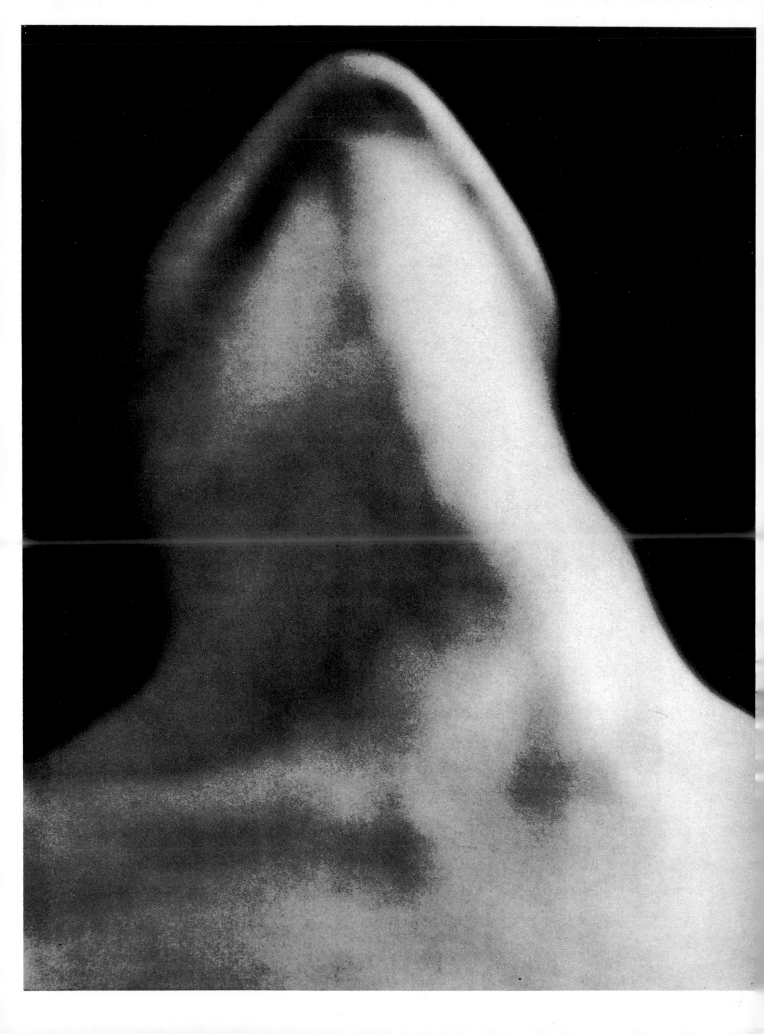

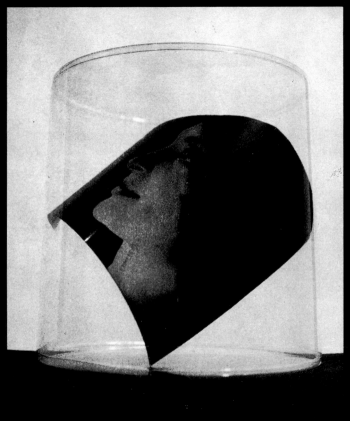

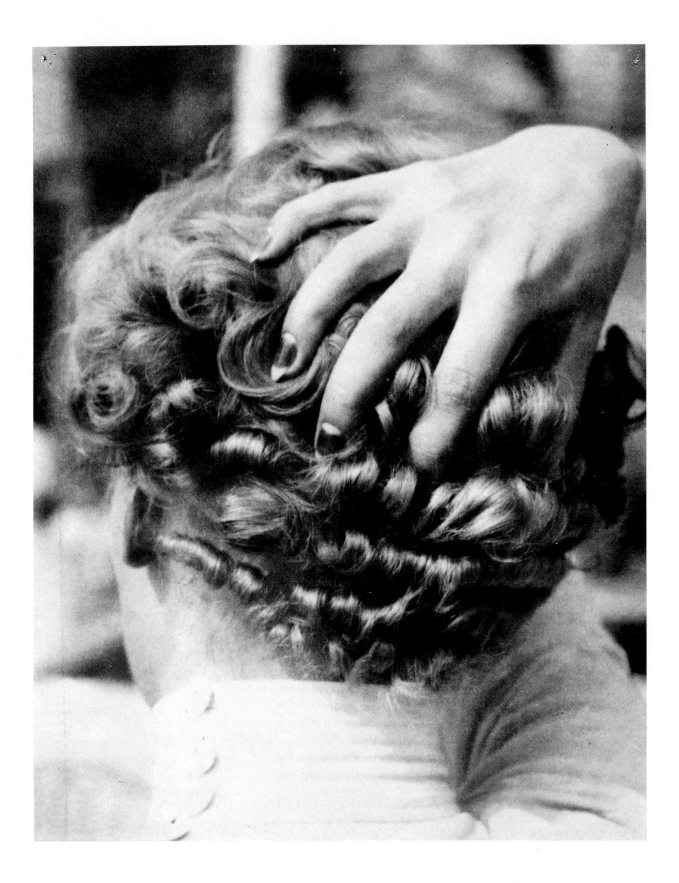

THE WHITE LADY, LA JOLLA, CAL.

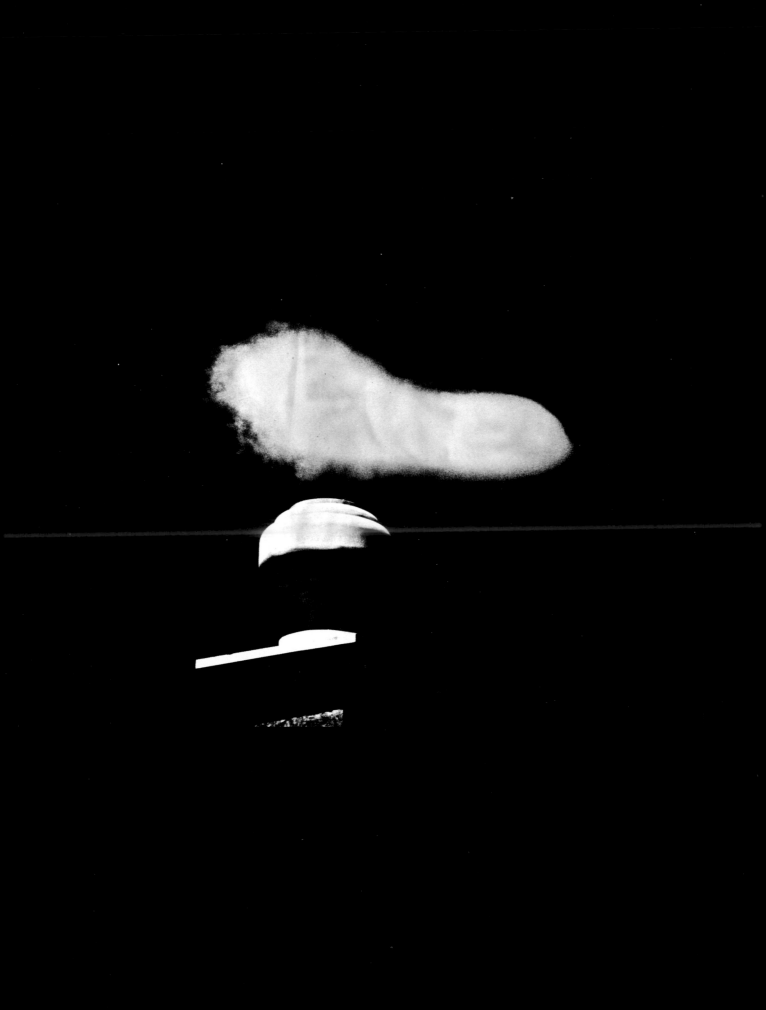

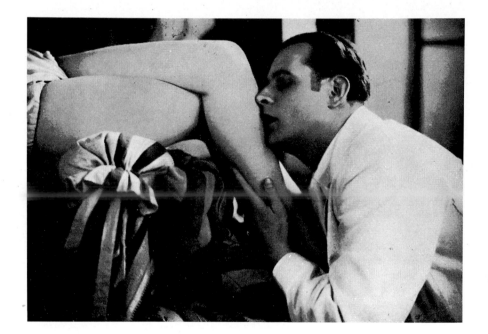

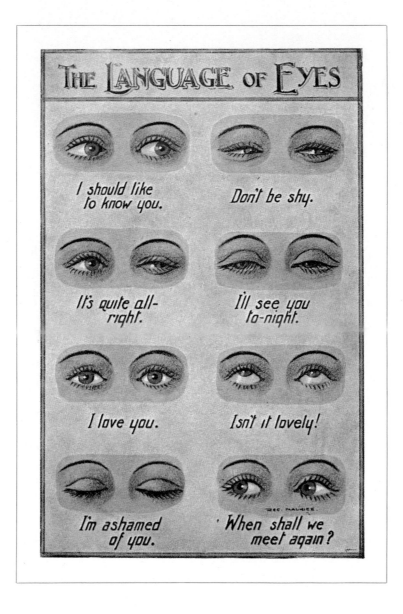

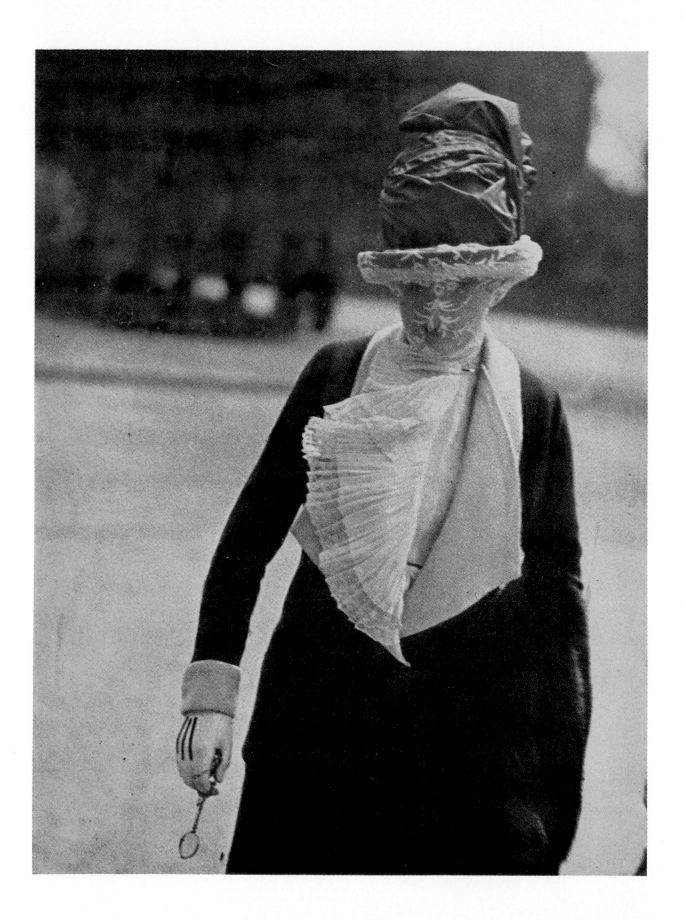

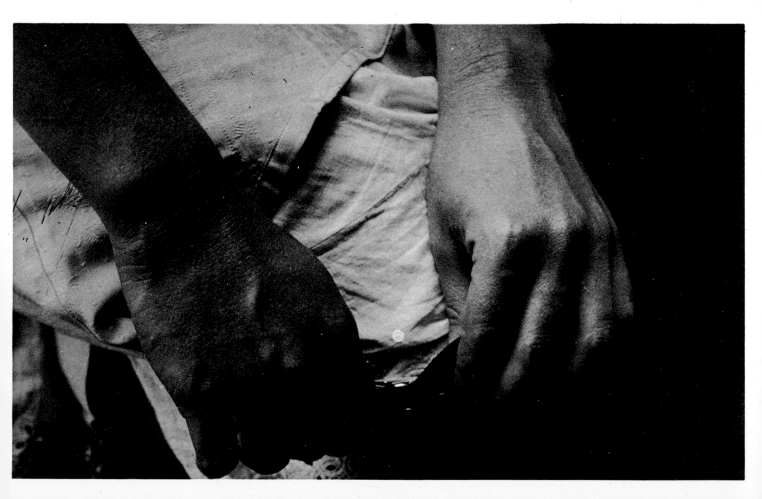

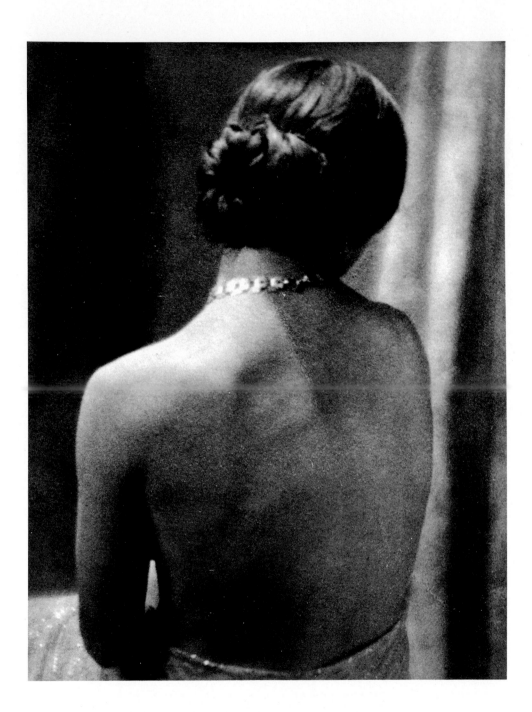

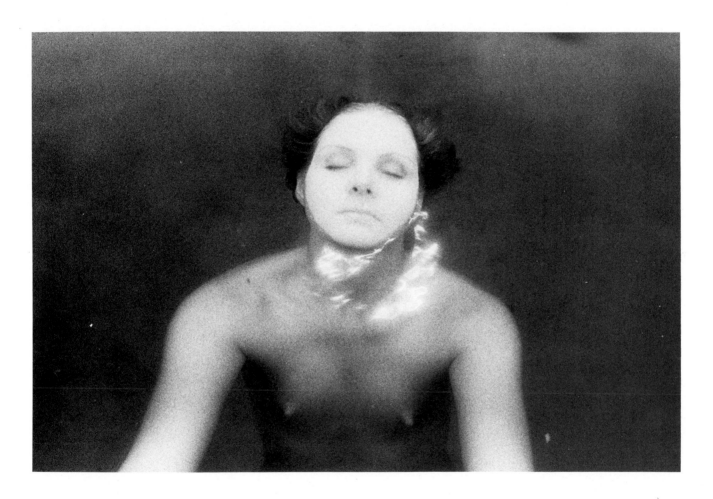

Who then, tells a finer tale than any of us? Silence does.   —Isak Dinesen

Anything which is entirely beyond my control fascinates me and seems to me to have some awful and particular significance, so that, while I was frightened, I was pleased also.   —Evelyn Scott

It's a question too complicated to answer...and too simple to ask.   —Penelope Gilliatt

In escorting me home we were obliged to cross a wide square, and in the commencement of our acquaintance, he always walked along the sides of the square; but I now saw that he simply traversed it in the middle, whence I concluded that his love had diminished in the same proportion.   —Mme. de Staël

Listening had been a large measure of her life: she listened closely—and since people are accustomed to being half-heard, her attention troubled them, they felt the inadequacy of what they said.   —Shirley Hazzard

Besides, when I say "nothing," what I mean is: everything.   —Isidora Aguirre

It was something to do with the sound...the way sound made images, shell within shell of them softly unclosing...the way words became colors and scents...and the surprise when it happened, the sense of fulfillment, the momentary perception of something unknowable....   —Rosamond Lehmann

"Don't you realize that the sea is the home of water? All water is off on a journey unless it's in the sea, and it's homesick, and bound to make its way home someday."   —Zora Neale Hurston

In a letter to Henri Mouder who had sent her a black lead drawing of a rose, Colette wrote: "I am looking at it through my magnifying glass, and thank God, I can discover nothing. You have left it all its mystery."

I suffer now—and suffered then—from moods which kept my head under water (so to speak) and only allowed me to see the things subjectively without enabling me to consider quietly the words of the other side.   —Anne Frank

I dwell in possibility.   —Emily Dickinson

It is as though God opened his hand and let you dance on it a little, and then shut it. . .so tight that you could not even cry.   —Katherine Mansfield

Opening the window, I open myself.   —Natalya Gorbanevskaya

"Why so silent?" said Her Majesty. "Say something. It is sad when you do not speak." "I am gazing into the autumn moon," I replied. "Ah yes," she remarked. "That is just what you should have said."   —*The Pillow Book of Sei Shonagon*

The silver question—is the one you are always afraid to ask (and the answer is yes).   —Debora Greger

Sometimes, surely, truth is closer to imagination—or to intelligence, to love—than to fact? To be accurate is not to be right.   —Shirley Hazzard

I was not looking for my dreams to interpret my life, but rather for my life to interpret my dreams.   —Susan Sontag

How strange everything is! When shall I see you? I don't know, but I shall see you. I am beginning to feel that faith that is given to people who fall off towers; they stay hovering for a moment in the air, in some comfortable and magical region where they feel no pain at all.   —Colette

Women never have young minds. They are born three thousand years old.   —Shelagh Delaney

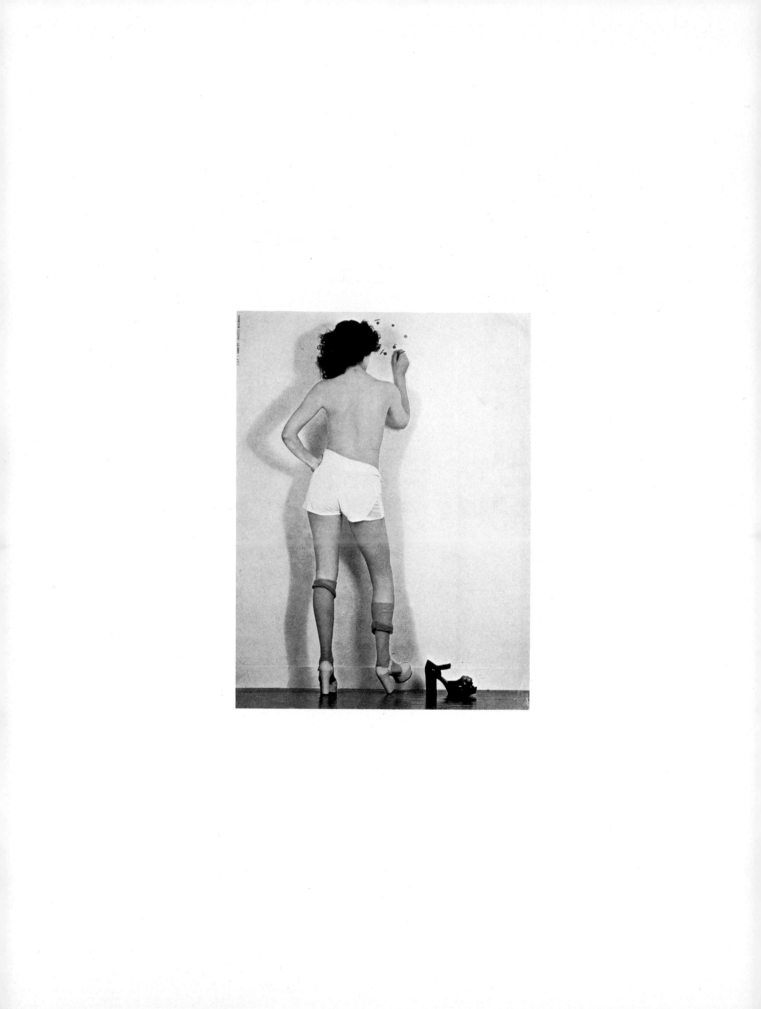

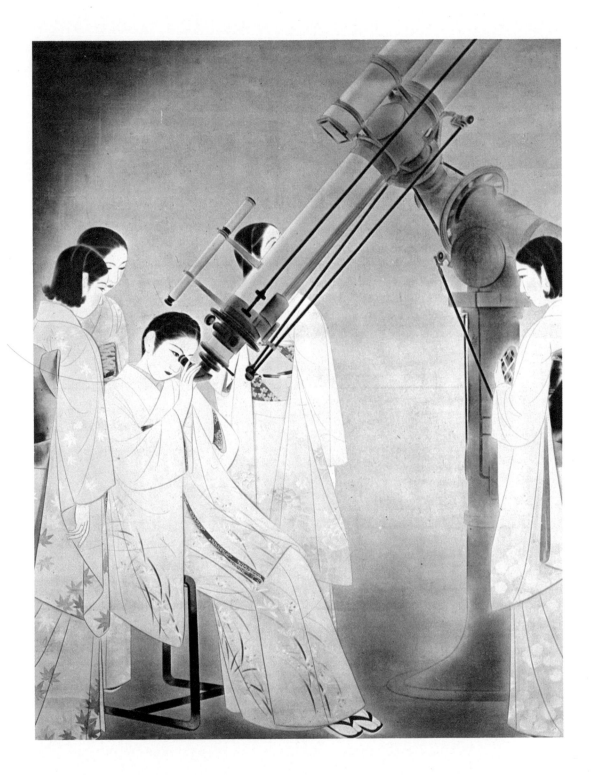

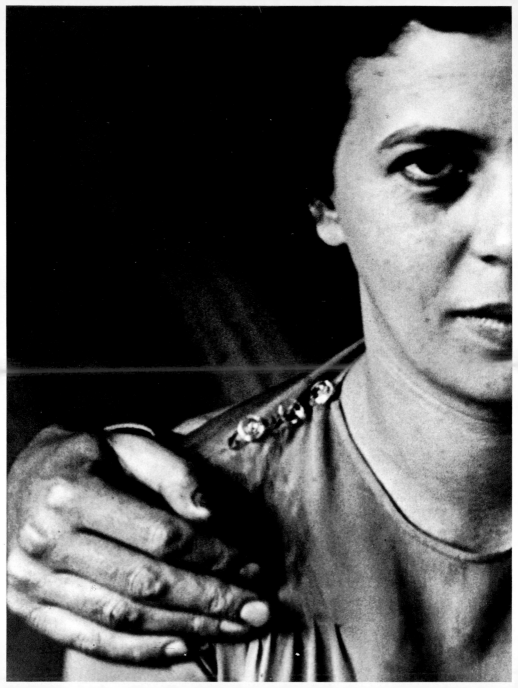

FIGARO
ILLUSTRÉ

Jacoves Wagrez.

For the womb has dreams. It is not as simple as the good earth.   —Anaïs Nin

I looked in my heart while the wild swans went over; and what did I see that I had not seen before? Only a question less or a question more; nothing to match the flight of wild birds flying.   —Edna St. Vincent Millay

I want something cool to press on all the places I'm burning. Ice roses beneath my hair.   —Lyn Lifshin

It is completely unimportant. That is why it is so interesting.   —Agatha Christie

I am sleeping inside the curves of the frozen zero.   —Sandra Hochman

My neighbor Howard says his mother saved everything. . . . His mother made little cloth bags to hold pieces of string, each bag carefully labelled as to the length of the pieces. After her death they found one small bag labelled "too short to save."

Come and get this food while it's hot.   —Iva Smith

In the garden I plant my hands. I know I shall grow, I know, I know. Swallows will lay their eggs in the nest of my fingers.   —Forugh Farrokhzad

When someone admired a nightgown she had bought in Paris, Djuna Barnes said, "Yes, I spent all summer looking for a night to go with that nightgown."

And me, I am writing a poem for you. Look! No hands.   —Ruth Krauss

That I will be strong enough to break in the right places. That broken I fulfill the wish.   —Debora Greger

All I can see from way back then is the light playing on the low ceiling and Mama's back bent over her sewing next to the lamp. I slept with my sister and she must have loved me 'cause I can remember on the coldest mornin's, she would get out of bed and warm my clothes next to the fire. When they were good and warm, she would stuff them under the quilts next to me so I could dress warm before getting out of bed.   —Irene Foster

Nothing would astonish me, after all these years, except to be understood.   —Ellen Glasgow

Now that I have your face by heart, I look. Now that I have your voice by heart, I read. Now that I have your heart by heart, I see.   —Louise Bogan

I realized a long time ago that a belief which does not spring from a conviction in the emotions is no belief at all. When I am convinced of something, I am convinced with my whole self, as though my flesh had informed me.   —Evelyn Scott

Return to the most human, nothing less will teach the angry spirit, the bewildered heart, the torn mind, to accept the whole of its duress, and pierced with anguish, at last act for love.   —May Sarton

Life must go on; I forget just why.   —Edna St. Vincent Millay

Remember it as a way out.   —Mary Hunter Austin

The Eskimos had fifty-two names for snow because it was important to them: there ought to be as many for love.   —Margaret Atwood

Femininity appears to be one of those pivotal qualities that is so important no one can define it.   —Caroline Bird

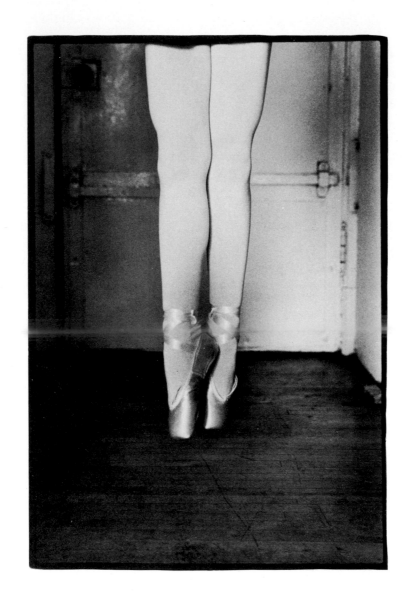

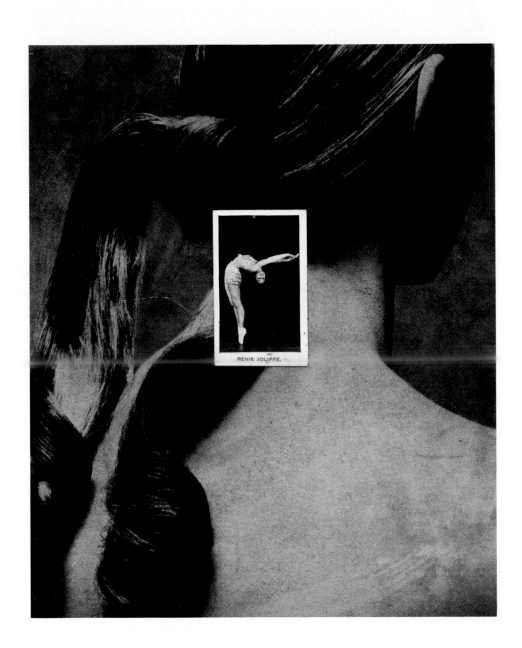

RENIE JOLIFFE.

NEW YORK'S FAVORITE SPRING and SUMMER MODELS...

MANY OTHER COLORS
SEE DESCRIPTIONS
ON OPPOSITE PAGE

(A) $1 29 POSTPAID

(B) $2 45 POSTPAID

(C) $1 88 POSTPAID

(D) $1 95 POSTPAID

(E) $2 45 POSTPAID

(F) $1 69 POSTPAID

(G) $1 95 POSTPAID

(H) $1 95 POSTPAID

(J) $2 45 POSTPAID

(K) $1 69 POSTPAID

(L) $1 69 POSTPAID

(M) $1 95 POSTPAID

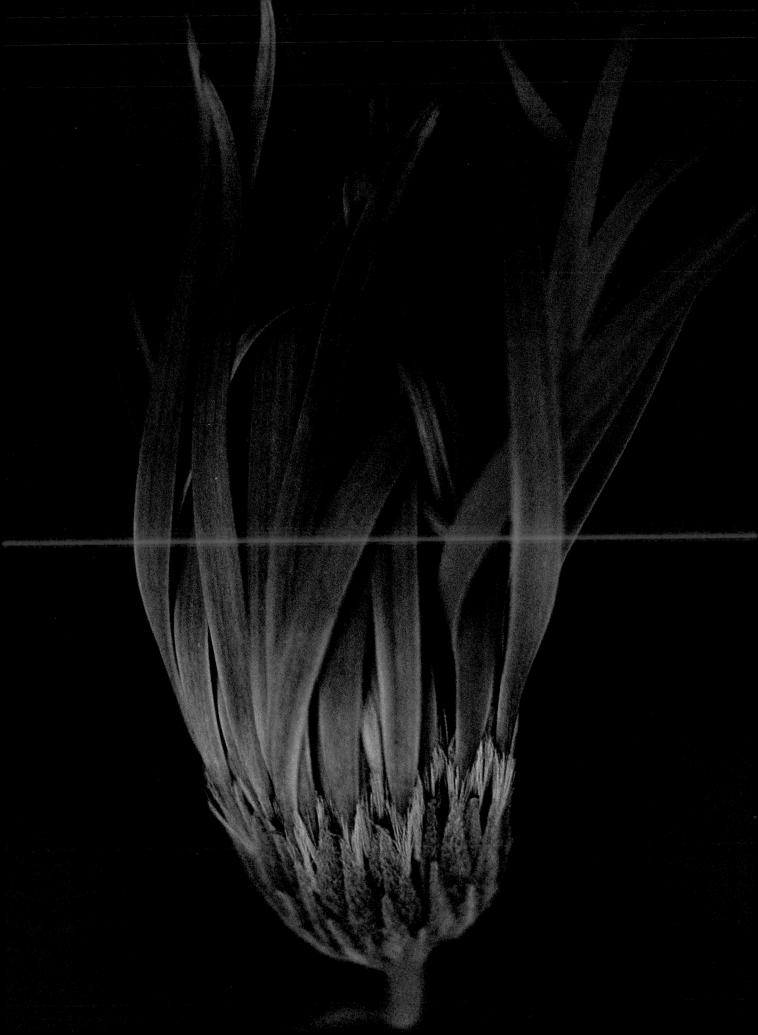

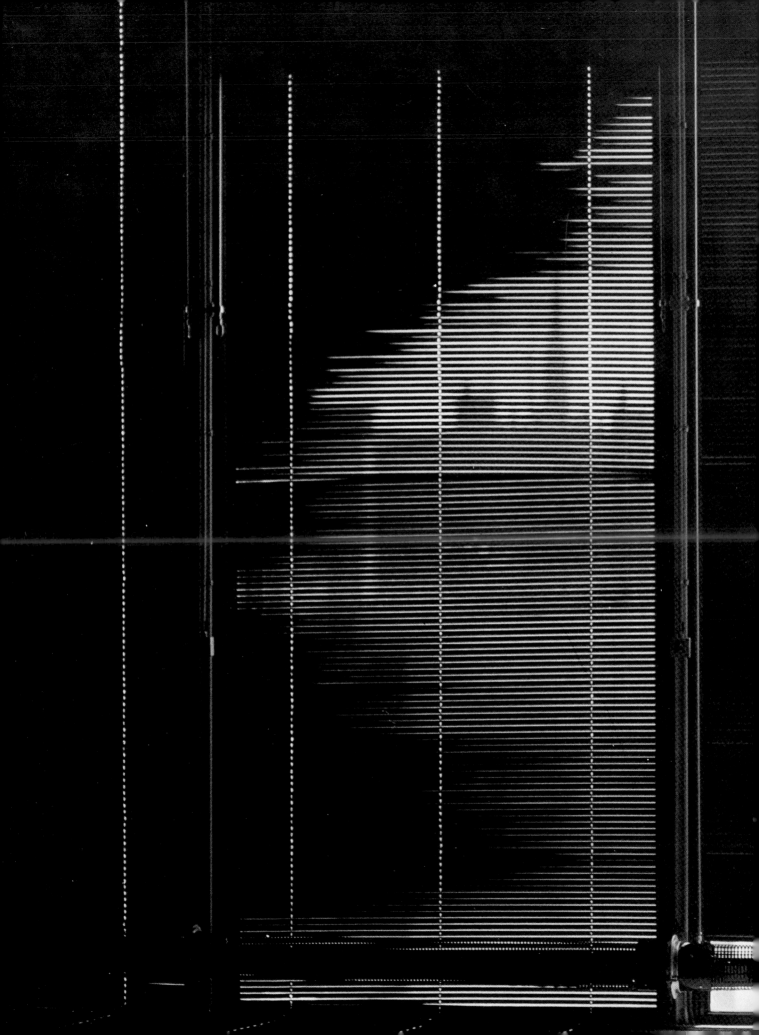

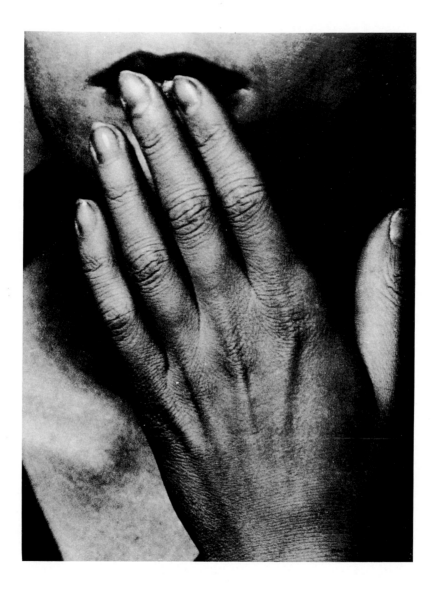

Boter man   Joncker

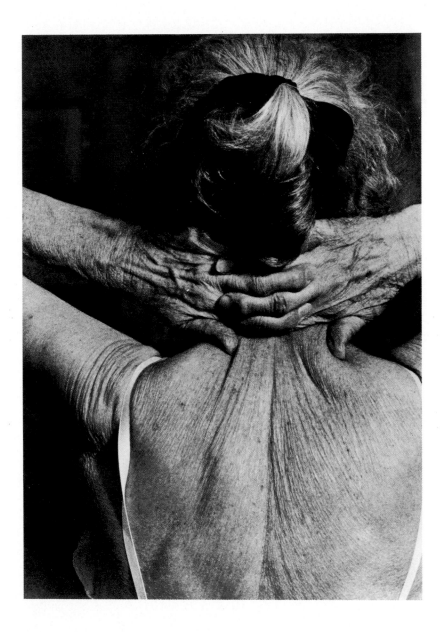

Printed at the Green Tiger Press, La Jolla, California

Bound by Lonnie's Trade Bindery, Lemon Grove, California

Color separations and black & white halftones were made at Photolitho, AG, Gossau-Zürich, Switzerland

Printed and bound in Hong Kong